A HAIRY CASE OF MURDER AT THE ANIMAL SANCTUARY

AN EMILY CHERRY COZY MYSTERY
BOOK THREE

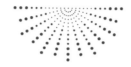

DONNA DOYLE

D1528789

PUREREAD.COM

CONTENTS

CHAPTER ONE

"Did you get enough to eat?" Emily Cherry glanced at the nearly empty dishes on the table before her. Their simple lunch of sandwiches and salads had been a very satisfying one for her, but she didn't want her guests to go away hungry.

"I ate it all, didn't I?" Nathan asked, tipping up his plate to emphasize the fact that he had nothing but crumbs left.

"Yes, but I guess I still remember how you were when you were a teen. Goodness, but you could eat! I thought I'd have to get a second job just to feed you," she laughed. It was hard to believe sometimes that her little boy was now the fully grown man in front of her, and he had been for quite some time.

"Trust me, if I ate anymore, I wouldn't fit into my suit tomorrow for work." He patted his stomach and pushed his chair away from the table. "I'll help you get these dishes cleaned up."

"That's sweet of you." Emily picked up her own plate and glanced at Genevieve, who hardly seemed to have heard a word of the conversation that'd taken place at the table. She was staring at her phone, her fingers swiping and tapping over the screen.

"Honey, were you done?" Nathan asked, nudging her salad bowl.

"Hm? Yes. I'm done." Genevieve only looked away from her screen long enough to glance at her husband before she was buried in whatever was so interesting on her phone again.

Nathan took her bowl and headed to the kitchen without saying a word.

Emily frowned. She and Genevieve had never been particularly close, although they'd always gotten along well enough. Emily didn't want to get involved in her children's relationships, and she knew that she didn't look at things the same way the younger generation did, but this was driving her crazy. "You know, there's an awful lot going on in the world that you're missing by being on your phone all the time," she said gently, hoping she could make her point without being offensive. She was working on being more assertive, but it wasn't an easy thing.

"This is for work," her daughter-in-law responded.

"Oh, I'm sorry," Emily said quickly. "I guess I thought you were on social media or something. And in any case, why are you working on a Sunday afternoon? Everyone deserves time to rest. That's the terrible thing about email and cell phones. Companies seem to think they can get a hold of their workers all the time these days, without any respect for the shifts they actually work." She'd heard some ladies in the grocery store complaining about just this sort of thing when one of them had been called in to work.

"I am on social media," Genevieve explained as she swiped her thumb across the screen. She turned it around to show Emily some of what she was looking at. "You see, being in the world of fashion doesn't simply mean designing a nice dress and hoping people will buy it. I have to stay ahead of all the coming trends and try to predict where they're going to lead. Engaging and networking with models, fabric creators, and other designers is essential to making a product hit the market with lots of momentum. Not to mention all the content creators and influencers. If just one top influencer reviews one of my products, our sales shoot through the roof."

Emily looked at Genevieve's phone, which to her didn't look any different from anything else she'd seen in her limited knowledge of social media. As far as she was concerned, it amounted to a few photos of someone eating or holding a cup of coffee in her hand. Emily didn't know what any of that had to do with fashion. "I see," she said, even though she definitely didn't. "You carry on then, dear."

Taking her dishes into the kitchen, she found that Nathan had already filled the washing up bowl with soapy water. Her phone dinged at her from the counter, but she ignored it. "You didn't have to do all that, you know."

"I don't mind. After all, you were the one who made dinner. There's no reason I can't help out a little bit, too."

Emily closed her mouth around a comment about Genevieve helping out as well. Rosemary strolled into the kitchen just then, shaking her puffy tail from side to side like she owned the place. She glanced at Nathan and immediately stood up on her hind legs, propping her front paws on the cabinet as she tried to see what she was doing.

"I'm afraid it's nothing very interesting," Nathan told the cat. "Just a little bit of wash."

"She's been quite the helper around here lately," Emily told him as she scraped a few tidbits of lettuce out of a bowl and put the condiments back in the refrigerator. Several more alerts sounded form her phone. "You should see her when I have my crafting supplies out! It starts innocently enough, and she's just batting gently at a few beads or sniffing some yarn. The next thing I know she's taking off down the hallway with a pipe cleaner in her mouth, yowling like she's caught herself a real prize!"

Nathan smiled. "You could teach her not to do those kinds of things, you know."

"I could try, but I doubt I'd be very successful." Emily patted Rosemary on the head before she grabbed a broom out of the closet to sweep up the floor. "She's involved in everything I do, and she has been ever since I got her. Besides, what's the point in having her if I'm just shooing her away all the time?"

"I guess that's true. At least she's a lot more pleasant than I thought she'd be when you got her. The only thing I've ever experienced with cats is that they scratch the curtains and leave hair on your clothes. I have to give Rosemary a pass considering how happy she makes you." He rinsed the last of the dishes and drained the water.

Rosemary, perhaps understanding that Nathan was being accepting of her, dropped back down to four legs and nudged the side of her head against his pantleg. Emily suppressed a laugh as she spotted a few hairs left behind on the fabric.

He was wiping his hands on a towel when her phone chimed once again. "Is that your phone? What's going on? I don't think I've ever heard it make so much noise."

"Oh, it's just my blog," she responded as she picked it up. Emily was finding that she enjoyed the experience of a cell phone more than she'd ever imagined she would, and she was able to find all sorts of help with apps and taking photos on the internet when she couldn't' figure something out. She did make it a policy, however, to finish whatever she was doing before she checked her notifications. The last thing she wanted was to be one of those people who lives more for that little electronic device than for the people around her.

"I guess it's doing well, then."

"It is," she confirmed, knowing that Nathan had initially doubted her ability to keep it going for so long. Emily smiled as she read the comments that had been left recently. "Right now, that's all thanks to Rosemary. When I was making some earrings the other day, she decided she wanted to help. She was in my way, and I think I lost more beads than I used, but she was so cute that I just had to take some photos. I figured it was still related to crafts, since she was playing with this string of yellow beads, so I went ahead and posted it. I've done that a few times now, and everyone seems to love them." She turned her phone around so Nathan could see the adorable picture of the cat.

His eyes immediately drifted down to the comments and other interactions underneath the snapshot. "You're getting quite a bit of traffic. You should take advantage of that and post as much as you can about Rosemary while she's a hot subject. There are quite a few websites and social media accounts that are about a pet, and I think a lot of them do quite well."

"Is that so?" Emily admired the photo once again. Rosemary's whiskers were always wild and crooked, and she thought it was an amusing contrast to the delicate, ladylike poses that cat favored. "I hadn't really thought about it."

"You should also think about monetizing your blog, if you haven't yet," he reminded her, bringing up a conversation they'd already had several times. "It might just be a few pence here and there at first, but if you do well enough you can actually supplement your income with it."

Irritation crinkled her brow, but she quickly smoothed it back out again. Nathan had been bugging her to do just that ever since she first mentioned starting a blog, and she knew he was only doing that because he cared about her and wanted her to have the best experience possible with it. She, however, was more interested in having fun and working her way towards writing a book. That had always been her dream, but the task sounded daunting. "Oh, I'll most likely do that sometime soon. But you're probably right about Rosemary. I'll have to get some more photos of her. It won't be hard. As soon as she hears me taking out the box of craft supplies, she right there in the middle of it!"

Rosemary had sat down in the kitchen doorway to groom her long, luxurious tortoiseshell fur. Sensing that she was being talked about, she placed her paws primly in front of her and blinked her big gold eyes, ready for her next photo shoot.

CHAPTER TWO

The next morning, as Emily sat in her favorite chair and sipped a couple of tea, her phone started firing off again. "You're such a popular girl, Rosemary," she noted pleasantly as she stroked her hand down the cat's back. Rosemary was firmly seated in Emily's lap. Their morning ritual of tea by the window that overlooked the garden was just as much her favorite time of day as it was Emily's.

Picking up her phone and seeing that there was another series of comments and likes on Rosemary's photo, Emily shook her head. "You know, I think Nathan is right. You're a hot commodity right now. Maybe it's because of those crazy whiskers you have, or perhaps your beautiful eyes. Either way, we ought to feature you more often."

Rosemary responded by snuggling a little further into Emily's lap, more interested in living the luxurious life of a housecat than worried about what strangers on the internet had to say.

"Not interested in photos today, huh?" Emily buried her fingers in the thick fur. The cat had been such a comfort ever since Sebastian passed away, and she didn't know how she'd ever get by without her. "That's all right. You know, something else I've always wanted to do was to write out your story. I know I wasn't there for it, but I think I remember every word the woman at the shelter told me when I came to see you. She told me all about how you'd been left behind at an abandoned house that was about to be knocked down. If it weren't for that contractor who'd decided to have one last look through the place to make sure there wasn't anything that could be salvaged, you might not be here today."

Emily chuckled a little to herself. "Apparently you scared the daylights out of him. He'd already been through the place several times, and he hadn't thought for a moment that there would be anybody in there. But you went darting through the room right in front of him to get back to your hidey-hole, and you were so fast he wasn't even sure what you were at first."

She scratched her fingernail along Rosemary's cheek. "I know it's a shame you had to live at the shelter for a while, but it was kind of him to turn you in to them. He could've just as easily decided to put you out the back door and call that good enough. What do you think, Rosemary? Would my readers want to know more about you?"

The cat flicked her tail.

Emily knew she should get up and grab her laptop while she was thinking about it. She was finding that the more time she spent on her blog, the more interested she was in writing. It was becoming one of her favorite activities, and it almost didn't matter what the subject matter was. She simply enjoyed the process of creating sentences and conveying ideas, and it was all the more satisfying to know someone out there was going to read it.

Right now, though, her mind was lost in that day she'd first gone to the shelter. She'd already decided she'd wanted a cat, and she'd left the house that morning with the idea that she'd simply go pick one out. It hadn't been that simple. There was such a variety of cats there, every one of them with a story, every one of them with a different personality. She'd known Rosemary was the one for her once they'd met, but what about all the others? It'd felt terrible to leave them behind, hoping that someone would come along for them someday.

"I do want to write that out, but I think there might be something else I need to take care of this morning. I'm sorry, honey." She gently picked the sleepy cat up out of her lap as she stood, turning around and putting Rosemary back down on the cushion before she went off to have a hunt through her house. She checked the drawer in the end table, flipping through some expired coupons and a nail file or two. Her desk was the logical place for it, but she only found her random notes about blog ideas and a few bills that she'd have to sit down and pay later. Just when she was about to give up, Emily walked into the kitchen and spotted them on the side of the fridge.

With the volunteer paperwork from Best Friends Furever in her hand, Emily returned to the living room. "Ms. Austin down at this shelter had said they need volunteers. I might not be able to give a home to every animal who needs one, but I can certainly help them out until they do find their homes. I'll just fill this out and run down there. I take it you'll be fine until I get back?"

Rosemary had resettled herself in the chair with her tail wrapped around so that it nearly covered her face.

"I thought so." Emily filled in the blanks, grabbed her keys, and headed across town.

Best Friends Furever had been the beneficiary of a craft fair Emily had attended, and then Emily had even worked with the director to create a whole new craft fair that would see the shelter getting a larger share of the profits. Emily had thoroughly intended to come back in and volunteer, but she'd gotten busy. There was no better time to start that now.

Lily Austin was behind the counter, tapping her pencil on the edge and chewing the inside of her cheek. She looked up when she heard the door, and a smile spread across her face. "Ms. Cherry! How nice to see you! What can I do for you?"

"Call me Emily, dear," she reminded her. "And I'm actually here about what I can do for you. It might've taken me a few months, but I've finally filled out my paperwork, and I'm reporting for duty." She slid the form across the counter.

"You're officially volunteering?" Lily's dark eyes brightened. "That's fantastic, and it couldn't have come at a better time. We're pretty short-staffed at the moment. One of the ladies who usually does quite a bit for us is having a surgery with a long recovery. We have a handful of paid workers, but one quit just yesterday morning and we haven't had many applications for the position. I'm afraid we can't afford very competitive pay, and that doesn't help."

"Well, you won't have to pay me a single pound. I'm just happy to be here. As I told you before, my cat came from a shelter. A different one than this, but thinking about her history has reminded me all over again of just how much these animals need our help." She felt so good knowing she'd make a difference in the lives of the animals here.

"Wonderful! Let's head into the cat room. I know you like cats, and they're all due to have their litter boxes scooped and their cages wiped down." Lily slipped Emily's paperwork into a folder and set it on the counter before heading off through a door.

Emily followed her, and she felt just as overwhelmed as she when Lily had first given her a tour of Best Friend

Furever. The long room was lined with cages all down each side and across the back, from the floor to about eye-level. There were even a couple of extra cages on casters that'd been wheeled into the room to provide space for litters of kittens. As soon as the pitiful creatures saw that someone had come in, they pressed their faces to the bars and meowed pitifully.

"Poor dear," Emily murmured as she put her finger inside one cage to scratch the forehead of a big orange cat.

"They should calm down as they get used to you," Lily explained. "I swear they know that there's a possibility of getting adopted when they see a person. Here's the supply closet for the room. You'll find fresh litter and scoops, and then you can use this spray cleaner and kitchen roll to wipe down the insides of their apartments. That's what I like to call them, anyway. It just sounds better."

"I completely agree," Emily said with a smile.

"There's an empty one over here, and you'll need to transfer each cat out while you clean their place, and then put them back. I don't think we have any right now that are particularly difficult or scratchy, but if you find that you have trouble with one, just let me know. Any questions?"

Emily looked at the long rows of kitty 'apartments.' It was going to be a daunting task, one that would undoubtedly leave her sore and tired by the end of the day. That didn't mean she was going to give up, though. "No, I think I can handle it."

"You're great! I'll be at the front desk if you need me." Lily left.

Now Emily was alone, except she wasn't alone at all. She had dozens of expectant cats looking at her, waiting to see what she wanted or what she was going to do. "Nothing to do but get started, right?" she asked as she turned to the first apartment in the top row on her left. It contained a skinny black cat who hovered like a shadow in the back corner of his cage. Emily glanced at the card attached the door. "My name is Enigma," she read out loud. "I was dropped off outside the building at night with no information. I'm a little shy, but I hope to find my family soon."

Frowning at the idea of the poor little thing being stuck in here without a family to love him, Emily very slowly opened the cage door so that she wouldn't scare him. "Hey, sweetheart. We're just going to move you right over here for a moment so we can get your place all cleaned up. All right?" She gently scooped him out and held him securely in her arms as she transferred him to the empty cage.

Enigma tensed up at first, pushing his paws against her chest and trying to get away. He quickly realized, though, that she wasn't going to hurt him, and he relaxed a little.

Lily poked her head back in half an hour later. "Everything going okay? None of them are giving you too much trouble, are they?"

"Oh, not at all!" Emily was cradling a fluffy cat in her arms, holding him like a baby and scratching behind his ears. "Butter doesn't seem to mind having his apartment cleaned as long as it means he gets a little bit of cuddling to go with it."

"I'm sure that's true," Lily laughed, giving Butter a scratch herself.

The big cat rumbled loudly.

"I noticed they all have a little story on their tags," Emily began. "I admit I've been spending some time reading about them, since I feel like my own cat's rescue story is important to her."

Lily gave her a sad smile. "I think it's important, too. They all have different backgrounds, different ways that they got here. My hope is that it'll help potential adopters understand that these aren't just plush animals you buy on a shelf in the store. They're real creatures with real feelings, and you can't just dump them off again when you're tired of them."

An idea had been brewing in Emily's mind. "I started a blog a while back, and I was wondering how you'd feel if I featured some of the animals here on it. I'm no professional by any means, and I can't even guarantee how many people would see the posts, but I'd like to help as much as I can."

"Of course!" Lily enthused. "I think it's a wonderful idea, and anything that can put them out into the world will help. Here, let me tell you a little more about Butter."

Emily began taking pictures and then taking notes as Lily told her all about the big cat's past, and she couldn't wait to put it all online.

CHAPTER THREE

"Have you seen my blue jacket?" Emily asked.

Rosemary twirled her tail against Emily's ankles but provided no further assistance.

She flipped through the crowded rack of hangers in the hall closet. "I swear I put it in here. In fact, I think I even remember doing it because it was so difficult to fit it back in with all this other stuff. "

"You know," Anita said in her headset, "you've hardly gotten rid of a thing since Sebastian died. I don't want to be the one to say it, but it might be time to start going through things."

"Oh, I don't know about that." Emily shoved aside a few other jackets, getting irritated that she couldn't find what she needed.

"I'd be willing to bet that you still have plenty of his things in that closet," Anita reminded her.

As she pushed aside one of Sebastian's old blazers, Emily scowled. "Well, maybe so. But it's nothing I have time to deal with today. I'm supposed to go to the shelter for my shift, and I'm going to be late."

"Can you be late for a volunteer position?" Anita queried.

Emily smiled and shook her head. Anita was a straight shooter. She didn't ever seem to care what other people thought, and she never hesitated to open her mouth. Folks often thought Emily would be that way, since she had the wild red hair that often accompanied that sort of personality, but she was still working on being as sassy as she'd like to be. "Yes, Anita. I may not be getting paid, but I made a promise. Those cats and dogs need all the help they can get. I love the work there, and I've barely even started."

Anita's tone softened. "You're really loving this, aren't you?"

"I am," she confirmed, feeling a special kind of warmth radiated over her face. "It's just so good to know that even if these pets don't have permanent homes yet, they have a clean healthy place to be in the meantime. And a few extra cuddles, of course."

"Of course."

"Rosemary, you be a good girl. I'll be back." Emily petted the cat before she left. "Anita, you be good, too."

"I'll try," her old friend joked. "If you get a call from the police, you'll know that they forgot to give me my senior discount at the café again."

When she reached Best Friends Furever, Emily bustled in to get started. "I'm so sorry I'm late! What do you need me to do today? Cat grooming? Dog walking?"

Lily was behind the counter once again, still frowning at her screen and wondering how she was going to pay all the bills. "Actually, I have something rather different to ask. And if you don't feel comfortable then you certainly don't have to do it."

Emily couldn't imagine anything that happened here that she wouldn't be willing to be a part of. "Of course. What is it?"

"Well, Millie needs to go to the vet."

"The sleek gray one in the apartment on the top row?" Emily had only worked at the shelter one day, but already she felt as though she knew each and every one of these sweet babies. Of course, getting to know their backstories had certainly helped with that. "Is there something wrong with her?"

"Yes, but nothing that can't be fixed. She needs a series of shots to get better and be healthy enough for adoption. I'd take her myself, but I'm mired in paperwork. It's so hard to get everyone to the vet when they need to go. And like I said, if you don't want to do this, then you certainly don't have to."

"It's not a problem at all," Emily insisted. "I take my own cat to the vet all the time, so I'm sure I can handle it. Just show me where the crates are and tell me which office to go to!"

A short time later, Millie was settled into a carrier on the passenger seat while Emily drove to Dr. Gallagher's office.

The building was a small and simple one, built fairly recently and set back from the road. Emily tucked her car into a parking space and headed inside. The waiting room was mostly taken up by the front desk, and Emily stepped up to it. "Hi, there! I've got Millie from Best Friends Furever here for her appointment."

The young man behind the desk sat slumped in his chair. He had one hand wrapped around a cup of coffee and the other one on a computer mouse, clicking away. The screen glowed on his glasses, keeping her from seeing his eyes, but Emily was quite certain that he wasn't bothering to look up at her.

"Clark, your coffee smells horrible!" a young woman pronounced as she stepped up behind the desk from one of the back rooms. "I don't know why you have to stink the place up with that when you're the only one who drinks it."

"Your loss, Lara." The young man just shrugged his shoulders and took another sip from his mug. He still hadn't said anything to Emily, and the brooding look on his face didn't suggest that she'd be getting help anytime soon.

"Did you need help?" Lara asked Emily, indicating the carrier in her hand.

"Yes. I have Millie from Best Friends Furever here for her appointment," Emily repeated, this time with far less enthusiasm.

Bending down to look at her own computer, Lara nodded. "All right. Dr. Gallagher will be with you in just a moment if you'd like to have a seat.

"Thank you." Emily sat in the row of chairs along one wall. There wasn't much room, but she squeezed in next to a lady with a nervous chihuahua. He sat in her arms and shook constantly, and Emily felt sorry for him.

It didn't take long before they were called back to an exam room, and Emily found out quickly that she liked Dr. Gallaher quite a bit. He acknowledged Emily, but his focus was entirely on the cat as he gently brought her out of her crate. He spoke softly as he listened to her heart and looked in her ears. "That's a girl. We'll get through all of this as quickly as we can," he crooned.

Finally, he looked back up at Emily as he stroked his wrinkled hand down Millie's back. "It looks like she's doing well overall, but she does need some shots. We'll get one today, but then she'll need to come back in a week."

"All right." Emily gently stroked Millie's ears while Dr. Gallagher gave the injection, talking softly to the cat and promising he would make it as quick as possible.

"All done!" he announced. "Stop in at the front desk and make sure you get an appointment card for the next injection. It needs to be in one week. I'll be out of the office, but Clark will be here."

Emily hesitated, not sure about the insolent young man.

"Since I've already looked Millie over and I know she's capable of handling the shot, he can do it," he assured her. "We have a small office here, so we often have to multitask between answering the phones and doing the actual hands-on work."

"I understand. That'll be fine."

"Also, I don't know if Ms. Austin told you, but the shelter is on a charge account with us. The shelter pets aren't the best paying clients, but they do always pay!" He laughed at his own joke.

"Thank you, Doctor. I know Millie appreciates everything you've done for her." Emily had decided that she liked Dr. Gallagher quite a bit. He obviously truly cared for his patients, and he didn't want them to be afraid while they were getting their treatment. If she didn't already have a vet she loved for Rosemary, then she would've made an appointment for her own cat.

Heading out into the lobby once again, Emily passed the woman with the nervous chihuahua and had a good feeling that the poor little guy would soon be feeling safe in the care of Dr. Gallagher. She was smiling as she stepped up to the counter, pleased with how the appointment had gone, but her smile faded a bit when she once again encountered Clark.

He was in the exact same position she'd seen him before, with his shoulders slumped forward and his hands fully occupied with his coffee and his mouse. It was the sort of position that Emily guessed the people at Mavis's tech firm probably took when they were figuring out some sort of software problem, intensely staring at the screen and completely oblivious to what was going on around them. That might be fine for that sort of corporation, but not here in a vet's office. People had questions, and they wanted to know their pets were being taken care of. It was a good thing she hadn't decided to change vets for the sake of Dr. Gallagher, because it would've meant dealing with Clark.

"Excuse me." She waited a moment, and when he didn't respond she glanced at his ears to see if she had a headset in. Emily had thought it rather strange when the Bluetooth headsets had become so popular and people would carry on their conversations even in the grocery store, but now that she'd had the experience herself, she could understand. There was no evidence of any devices like that, though. "Excuse me? I need to make an appointment for next week."

"I've got you." Lara waved her over. "How about ten o'clock?"

Emily didn't know if she should check with Lily, but it certainly worked for her own schedule. She'd just tell the shelter director that she'd make sure she brought Millie in herself so there would be no risk of conflicts. "That would be fine, thank you."

Lara handed over an appointment card. "Have a great day!"

"Now you see," Emily said to Millie when they got back in the car, "that's how it should be done!"

CHAPTER FOUR

"Mom, it's wonderful!" Phoebe gushed over the phone. "I always make sure I read your blogs, but the ones about the pets are just amazing!"

"You think so?" Even though nobody could see her at the moment but Rosemary, Emily felt herself blush. It was nice to know that her middle daughter read her work, and it was even better to get praise for it. She'd always viewed this as a hobby, and she knew it would never be anything beyond that, but it was enough to let her know she ought to keep going.

"I do. These poor little cats! The way you write their stories makes them seem like something out of a book or a movie. I have to be careful when I share it all with Lucy and Ella. If they just see the photo, they make cutesy noises over the pretty kitty and move on. But if they knew these stories, they'd probably have me bringing every single one of them home."

"Trust me. I understand the problem!" Emily had her cat. She didn't need any more, and she didn't want Rosemary to feel like she had to compete with another cat. Still, she hated to know that they were on their own in the world. She was helping them, and in more ways than one, but sometimes it didn't seem like enough.

"They've already been asking for a pet ever since Mavis adopted Gus. He's adorable, and I've entertained the idea, but I'm just not sure at the moment. We already have a lot going on."

"You have to do what's right for you," Emily insisted. There were animal advocates who would tell nearly everyone that they ought to adopt a stray, whether out of want and need or simply pure moral obligation. Emily didn't quite agree with that, though. The pet's needs should also be considered. "They need a place where they're wanted and loved, and it's perfectly all right if you don't have the time right now. You might later. Don't think there's any pressure from me just because I'm spending time over there."

"Thanks. I do think it's wonderful that you're doing this, Mom. Both the work at the shelter and what you're posting online."

Emily laughed. "I think I enjoy the online part a lot more than I thought I would! I do love writing out their stories after I find out all the details from Lily. Then there are all the comments that come in! Since I put on there that I'm volunteering, they ask me questions about the cat's personality and if they get along with dogs. It's so nice to sit down in the evening with Rosemary in my lap and chat with them." She hadn't ever imagined getting that sort of satisfaction out of a blog, but she definitely was lately.

"I'd better go. I've got some errands to run before I pick Ella up from preschool."

"That's all right, dear. I've got to do some things myself." Emily glanced at the clock, realizing that she was once again nearly running late. She headed off to the shelter, shaking her head at herself. She hadn't ever been late when she still worked for Phoenix Insurance. In fact, she'd taken it as a point of pride to always be there at least a little on the early side. She could cut herself some slack since she was retired now, but she'd still much rather be early than late.

It didn't take long to get Millie in her crate and head right back out of the shelter toward Dr. Gallagher's office. When she pulled into the parking lot at the vet's office and saw only one car, she remembered what the vet had told her. "I'm afraid you'll have to deal with Clark today, sweetheart," Emily said to the cat, trying to reassure her though the bars of the crate. "I know he didn't exactly have a great personality when we were here last time, but the only thing that's really important is that we get the job done. If he's as cranky and unsociable as he was last time, then I promise I'll get you an extra treat when we get back to the shelter. Well, I probably will anyway."

Millie let out a small meow as Emily took the carrier out of the passenger seat.

"That's right. I can even let you pick. I think there's tuna or chicken flavor, so you've got some time to think about it." She headed into the office, hoping she could get more response from the rude young man than she had last time.

"Good morning," Emily said as she opened the door. There wasn't anyone else waiting on the row of chairs along one wall as there had been last time. She assumed this was because Clark was here alone, and there were only so many things he could do. They might be able to schedule some injections, but probably nothing more in-depth than that. Nearly tripping over the rug, Emily looked down as she wiped her feet. "I've got Millie here for her shot today."

When there was no response from Clark, Emily looked up and glared at the top of his dark head over the counter. He couldn't even bother to acknowledge her! She marched forward, determined to give him a piece of her mind. "Listen, I…"

Emily trailed off when she realized something was terribly wrong. Clark was slumped over his desk once again, but this time he was a little too far forward. One hand was still on the computer mouse, the other around his cup of coffee, but he didn't look like he'd be looking at the screen or taking a sip any time soon.

"Clark?" She reached over the counter and pressed her fingers to his neck, wishing she didn't have to. It told her what she was already thinking, though. She set the cat carrier on a nearby chair and fished her phone out of her pocket with shaking hands. "I've got a phone call to make, Millie. Just hang on a minute."

The police arrived quickly, flooding into the tiny building and taking charge. Chief Inspector Woods was there himself, and Emily remembered him well from her little incident at The Silver Swan. "Ma'am, why don't you come right on back here with me?" he said, taking her by the elbow. "You can bring your kitty, too."

Wonderful. He was going to be just as condescending as he had been before. "She's not mine, actually. I'm doing volunteer work for the shelter, and I just brought her in for her appointment."

Woods led the way to an exam room at the back, one that the police had already gone through to make sure there wasn't any evidence to preserve. "That's very sweet of you. And now you've had a terrible scare, I'm sure. I'm going to need to ask you some questions, but I've got a few other things to take care of first. Do you mind waiting here for me?" The patronizing tone of his voice made him sound as though he were talking to a small child.

Emily wished Alyssa were here to handle the case instead, but she was stuck with things the way they were. "I'll be perfectly fine," she assured him confidently. "You take your time."

Chief Inspector Woods left, closing the door gently behind him. As soon as he was no longer talking to Emily, he took on the strong, commanding voice that his position required as he spoke to his officers. "You said Dr. Gallagher is here? Good. I'll be speaking with him in the first exam room. Let me know if there's anything I need to see." Next came the sound of a door opening and closing.

Emily settled in on the chair that was put in the room for pet owners, even though she'd often found that there was rarely a chance to sit in it when she was in with either her own cat or one from the shelter. She always felt as though the right thing to do was stand up and comfort the pet on the exam table, so it felt strange to just be sitting there in the corner with the carrier at her feet.

"Dr. Gallagher, I'm sure you're aware by now that we've found your vet tech, Clark Gibson, deceased at the front desk."

Emily's head snapped up. The exam rooms were right next to each other, and she could hear every word through the thin walls. She knew she probably shouldn't listen, but how could she not?

"I am. Oh, this is so terrible. Do you know what happened?"

"That's what we're trying to figure out," Woods replied sharply. "I'll need information from you for that. Have you been to the office at all this morning?"

"No, sir. I had the day off because of my family reunion. Nobody was going to be here but Clark. There were a few small appointments he was going to do, basically just administering medication and a few injections. But I came in as soon as you called me."

"I see." Woods paused for a moment, and Emily imagined he was looking through his notes. "Mr. Gibson seems to have died rather suddenly. There aren't any external injuries, which indicates that it may have been natural causes, but he was a relatively young man. I don't want to completely rule out foul play until we've examined every aspect of this. Was there anyone who might wanted to have hurt Clark? Someone who would've like to see him dead?"

It was easy to imagine the shocked look on Dr. Gallagher's face. He was such a sweet old man, and Emily hated that he was having to think about this. He didn't respond for a long moment. "Not that I'm aware of," he finally said, softly enough that Emily had to get up out of her chair and press her ear against the wall to be sure she was getting all of it. "I'm afraid that I was being blackmailed, however."

"Tell me more about that," Woods quickly fired back.

"I made a mistake a few months ago. It was a simple mix-up of giving a patient the wrong medication when a bottle was mislabeled. I was able to identify what happened and remedy the problem, and I didn't charge the patient a thing, of course. The owner was understanding, I thought, but more recently I've been getting threats. I've had to shell out some money to keep them quiet. It was a simple mistake, but not the kind I really want to get out into the public. It could ruin my business."

"Are these threats coming from the owner in that particular incident?"

"I have no idea, to be honest with you. I'm happy to give you any information I can." Dr. Gallagher hesitated. "You see, I recently stopped making the payments this person asked for. I really can't afford it. We're a small-town office, and I want to charge prices that I know people can afford so that they'll take good care of their animals. But now I'm terrified that someone came here to get revenge on me, and Clark got in the way."

Emily stepped back from the wall. She tapped her fingers against her lips and paced the small amount of space in the room for a moment, unsure of what to do with herself. She knelt down to check on the cat. "It sounds like things are getting interesting, Millie."

CHAPTER FIVE

"A re you sure you're up for this?" Lily's pale brows scrunched up over her dark eyes. She held Millie in her arms, rubbing her fingers over the short gray fur.

Emily nodded. "I'm sure."

Lily bit her lip. "It's just that I know you've already been through a lot. I can't imagine how you must feel, and I don't want you to have to put yourself back in a position that might make you feel that way again."

"When I signed up as a volunteer, I knew that the work wouldn't always be easy. What happened yesterday at Dr. Gallagher's office is regrettable, but I'm sure things will be completely different at this other vet office. Millie still needs her shots, and I want to help her out. If Dr. Gallagher's office is closed for the investigation, then we just have to carry on." Emily lifted her chin in the air a little bit, wondering if she looked even a fraction as confident as Anita did when she was telling someone how things were going to be.

One side of Lily's mouth twitched. "I have to tell you, Emily, I don't think I've ever had a volunteer who's as dedicated as you are. You've only been her a week, but you're here every time you say you're going to and you're always so full of energy. I can't tell you how much I appreciate that."

Emily took Millie from the shelter director's arms and nestled her safely into the carrier. "It's for them. I know someone had to take care of my Rosemary before I came along and adopted her, and now I want to return the favor."

"Is Rosemary jealous of all the time you've been spending here?" Lily double-checked that the sticker on the carrier had Millie's name and the shelter's number.

"She has been a little more cuddly than usual," Emily admitted, thinking of how insistent Rosemary had been about jumping up in her lap and snuggling as soon as she sat down the previous evening. She'd pushed her face up under Emily's hand, insisting on lots of pets, and then she'd even dug her claws in a little when Emily had attempted to get up to go to bed. "I'll have to make sure I give her lots of extra attention. I don't want her to feel like she's second-best!"

"Dr. Cunningham is over on Marshall. She's a good vet, although she's got a very different personality from Dr. Gallagher. We've used her a few times before when Dr. Gallagher was on vacation, so she's familiar with us," Lily explained.

"I'm sure it won't be a problem at all. We'll be back as soon as we can!"

Dr. Cunningham's office was nothing at all like Dr. Gallagher's. It was a large building that looked rather new and well-made. Even the parking lot was practically perfect, with hardly a crack to be seen. Inside, it was all bright lights and new paint. The waiting room was spacious, and a large fish tank took up one entire wall. Emily raised her eyebrows, wondering how many cats went wild trying to catch the flashes of tropical color. Even the scent in the air was surprising, because the place smelled more like fresh laundry than pets.

"Hello, and welcome to Cunningham Veterinary," a woman said sweetly from the front desk. She was sitting up straight and making eye contact, the complete opposite of Clark. "Can I have the patient's name, please?"

Even though she felt bad about judging someone who was no longer of this earth, Emily had to appreciate how much better at her job this young woman was. "This is Millie, from Best Friends Furever."

One quick glance at her screen told her everything she needed to know, and she pointed to a row of padded chairs. "I'll get her checked in. You can have a seat right over there, and someone will be with you shortly!"

"Shortly" wasn't an exaggeration. Emily's backside had hardly even touched the cushion before a woman in scrubs was calling Millie's name from a nearby doorway. "Come right on back to Exam Room 3, please."

The hallway wasn't as fancy as the lobby, but Emily was still impressed as she realized just how big this place was. Even Millie was looking around with interest, sniffing the air.

The vet tech settled them into a room, took Millie's vitals, and then left with a promise that Dr. Cunningham would be in right away. This place was a model of efficiency, since it was hardly more than a minute that they waited. Dr. Cunningham was a young woman in her mid-thirties. She carried a laptop as she walked in, and she was frowning at the screen, but she set it down to shake Emily's hand and introduce herself. "I'm Dr. Cunningham. I take it you're from the shelter?"

"One of its newest volunteers," Emily explained.

The vet's dark brows shot up near her short hair as she turned around to wash her hands at the small sink. "That's a surprise. Most places like that can hardly recruit anyone even if they pay them."

"I enjoy the work." It was true, but it was a shame that she had to keep explaining it so much. Shouldn't everyone like helping others?

The doctor opened the carrier door and coaxed Millie out, quickly and efficiently examining her. Though she wasn't taking nearly as long as Dr. Gallagher did, nor did she whisper and talk to the cat while doing her job, it was still nice to see that she also was putting the patient first. "I understand this little girl had been seeing Dr. Gallagher?"

"That's correct. His office is...closed at the moment." Emily wasn't sure how else to put that.

Dr. Cunningham nodded. "So I heard. I can't say that I'm surprised, though."

"No?" Emily blinked. The vet may not have been surprised, but she certainly was! She hadn't expected their conversation to go beyond the cat in question.

After listening to Millie's heart, Dr. Cunningham pulled her stethoscope back down around her neck. "Not at all. You see, Clark Gibson used to work in this office."

"Really?" The surprises just kept on coming. It was hard to imagine someone like Clark working in a nice, friendly office like this. He certainly wouldn't have acted the way the receptionist at the front had.

"Oh, yeah." Dr. Cunningham stroked her hands down Millie's back for a moment before she turned away from the exam table and began rummaging in a drawer. "Not for very long, mind you. He wasn't that great of an employee. I suppose I shouldn't say that, considering that he's dead, but it's true."

"Did you fire him?" Emily supposed she shouldn't say *that,* but she wasn't the one who'd started the conversation. If the vet was willing to talk, then she was more than willing to listen.

"I sure did." Dr. Cunningham let out a small laugh as she filled a syringe. "He attempted to blackmail me."

Emily couldn't believe what she was hearing! What were the chances that both Dr. Gallagher and Dr. Cunningham had been blackmailed? Was someone making a living out of finding out the secret lives of veterinarians? It seemed pretty far-fetched to her. "That does seem like something you'd fire a person for."

"I agree. You see, he wanted to expose me for having what he believed was an affair. He'd seen me out in the parking lot after work when my boyfriend would pick me up or drop me off from lunch. I'd gotten divorced from my husband shortly before Clark began working here, and we were keeping up appearances to a degree because we both owned the business. We simply didn't want everyone asking us what was going on until we knew all the answers. Clark didn't know any of that, and he just assumed that I was doing something I shouldn't be. He had the audacity to come straight to me and tell me all about how he was going to expose me unless I doubled his salary. I fired him on the spot." Dr. Cunningham gave Millie her injection between the shoulder blades, and the cat hardly seemed to notice.

"I can't say that I blame you. I think you're pretty brave for flat-out refusing him." She wondered if she'd be able to do this should someone come to her with such an ultimatum. Dr. Gallagher had eventually refused to make payments to his blackmailer, but it sounded as though it'd taken him some time.

Dr. Cunningham waved off the compliment as she scooped Millie up off the table and held her close. "Oh, no. It really wasn't brave of me at all. I was actually shaking so hard I could barely keep my voice calm. I was livid, and I was even a little scared. I mean, what kind of a nut does that to his own boss?"

"Indeed."

"Here you go, sweetie." The vet put Millie back in her carrier and gave her a few more pets before she gently closed the door. "She should be all good to go for the next week. I would imagine Dr. Gallagher's office will be opened back up by then, but if not just give us a call. We'll be sure to work it in."

"Thank you very much for everything." Emily stopped in at the front desk, where the receptionist chirped happily to her about the possibility of an appointment for next week, and then she was back out in her car.

"All right, Millie. You'll have to tell me what kind of treat you want today. You were a very good girl, and you certainly deserve it."

"Meow."

Emily turned left onto the main road. "Tuna? Sounds good. What did you think of what Dr. Cunningham said about Clark?"

"Me-ow-ow."

"My thoughts exactly," Emily confirmed. "I'd initially thought someone was trying to blackmail Dr. Gallagher, got angry with him when he refused to pay them anymore, and then Clark got in the way. Now I'm starting to realize that Clark was the one who got himself wrapped up in this. He already tried to coerce Dr. Cunningham. It hadn't worked for her, but it certainly had with Dr. Gallagher for a time. If he was the blackmailer, then who killed him?

CHAPTER SIX

"It seems a little extra loud in here today." Emily stood in the dog kennel. This area was essentially like a long hallway, with large cages all the way down on both sides. Each one had food and water bowls, a cot, a drain, and even access to a small run. It was better than some of the conditions she'd seen in other shelters, but the dogs still seemed to have plenty to say about it. They jumped up and pushed their paws against the chain link fencing of the cages, their howls and barks emphasized by the concrete and metal construction.

"Well, we do have an extra tenant for the moment. I'm hopeful that he's temporary." Lily strode down the long hall until she found one of the last doors on the left. "This is Diesel. He belonged to Clark Gibson."

Emily looked through the chain link door at the big black dog. He had a body like a barrel, with thick stumpy legs and a wide head. Unlike the other dogs in the shelter, he didn't throw himself at the cage door and bark for attention. Instead, he sat in the very center of the kennel, watching them with dark eyes. Diesel looked like he was waiting for something to happen.

Her mind was churning as soon as she heard who his owner had been. "How did the poor little guy end up here? Didn't any of his family want him?"

Lily shrugged. "I guess Clark had brought Diesel to work with him the day that he died. Dr. Gallagher found him in the back and called me because he wasn't sure what else to do with him."

"Oh, interesting. I wonder if Diesel saw anything that day." She didn't remember seeing the dog out in the lobby when she'd brought Millie in for her shot that day, but she did fully believe that pets were observant creatures who knew right from wrong and good from bad. She would certainly trust Rosemary's instincts if there was someone she didn't like.

"I don't think so," Lily replied. "He was in the back. Clark's roommate Mason has agreed to take him, but there's one problem. Mason's car is in the shop, and I don't think Diesel will cooperate enough to let anyone take him over there."

"What do you mean?" Emily looked at the placid dog. "He seems fine."

"Sure, until you do this." Lily lifted the latch and opened the door. The dog was instantly on all four feet and growling. She shut the cage, and he sat down once again. "The poor guy has a hair trigger. He even bit Lara over at Dr. Gallagher's office."

Emily had to wonder what sort of training Clark had given this dog if he was so defensive. "Can I try?"

"Oh, I really don't know that you should do that," Lily warned. "I don't want you to get hurt. How will we get on here without our favorite volunteer?"

"Let's see just how much of a favorite I am." Her stomach tightened a bit, but Emily reached over and lifted the latch. Diesel was watching her carefully. Emily stood there for a long moment, letting him get used to the one small change she'd made by just lifting that tiny piece of metal out of the way. Then, so slowly that it made her impatient with her own movements, she swung the gate open.

It wasn't as though Lilly had flung the door open and startled him before, but Emily's technique did seem to be helping. He was standing up on all fours, and he was watching closely, but at least he wasn't growling.

"That's a good boy," Emily purred, thinking of the way she'd always had to speak so softly to Rosemary when she'd first brought the cat home. Shelter animals were living in loud, chaotic environments, and even coming to a nice quiet home was a big adjustment. Emily's knees

43

creaked as she squatted down so that she was on eye level, but she didn't attempt to come into the cage. "I just want to help you out, sweetheart. I hope you'll let me."

Diesel tipped his head to the side as he watched her slowly extend her arm. He stretched his head forward and sniffed the air. For a few seconds, Emily wasn't sure that this was going to do any good, but she knew she had to try. This poor dog had lost his owner, and no matter how rude Clark had been, and he was hurting. Finally, Diesel stepped forward and sniffed her fingers before butting his head up under her palm.

"Well," Lily chuckled, "I guess you really are the favorite volunteer around here!"

Emily's heart was filled with warmth as she scratched behind Diesel's ears and under his chin. "I never really thought of myself as a dog person, but this guy might be changing my mind. I can take him over to Clark's roommate."

The director's attitude quickly changed back to one of doubt. "It's one thing to pet him, but it's another to be in a car with him by yourself."

"I'll be all right." Emily didn't know how she knew, but she knew. She unclipped a leash from next to the gate. "You want to go for a ride, boy?"

Diesel's tail was whipping back and forth so hard that it seemed to be wagging his body instead of the other way around.

"All right. But do be careful. I'll get the address." Lily headed back toward the office.

"What a good boy you are, even if you are getting hair all over the seats," Emily laughed as she buckled herself into the driver's seat a few minutes later.

Diesel looked out the windows, his little brows stretching up in concern.

"It's all right." Emily spoke calmly and gently, knowing how much it helped Rosemary when she was in the car. It didn't really matter what she said. It was more of how she said it. "We're going to get you back home. I know your owner won't be there anymore, and that's going to be tough, but at least you'll get to live in the same place."

Diesel's head was drooping as he glanced out the window, still uncertain.

"You get to see a lot of things on the way. All the birds and trees." Emily remembered talking to her children like this when they were little. It was a constant chatter of the world around them, and they had learned to speak better than most children by the time they entered school. "I have to wonder if you saw anything the day that Clark died. I mean, you were there at the office with him. There weren't any other people. You might know more than anybody, and it's frustrating that we can't ask you. I know they'd never accept your testimony in court, of course, but I still think it'd be interesting to hear your side of the story."

Diesel once again looked just as solemn as he had when she'd first seen him in his cage at the shelter.

"All right. I'm sorry. I can perk the conversation back up a little bit. We don't have to talk about such heavy things, and I certainly don't blame you. I don't think I'd want to, either. Oh, look. There's a new building going up over there. That sort of thing always makes me wonder what sort of business they'll be putting in. I hope it's something fun that my friend Anita and I can go check out, maybe a clothing shop or a thrift store. You might like Anita. She's very direct, but that means she's always honest."

Diesel's chest expanded as he took a deep breath and then let it out as a heavy sigh.

"I know. I'm sorry, buddy. Do you see that big blue sign over there for Dorris Financial consultants? My husband Sebastian used to get called out for insurance estimates on their fleet vehicles all the time. He was an insurance adjuster, you see. It was his job to figure out how much damage had been done after an accident. He liked that sort of work, pricing out all the little bits and pieces it would take to put a vehicle back together again and then figuring out how long it would take. I think Dorris Financial alone kept him in a job, considering how many accidents they had. It became a joke between the two of us that they needed to start hiring people who knew how to drive instead of people who knew how to handle money!" She laughed at the fond memory of her late husband.

Diesel's ears perked up. His tail was wagging again, although in the small confines of the car he didn't have the space to do it with as much enthusiasm as he had before. His entire demeanor had changed once again.

"I guess you liked that story?" Emily asked. "I've got plenty more for you."

Now Diesel was up on his feet in the seat, and she had to reach over and push his back end down so that he wouldn't fall and get hurt. He was whipping his head back and forth and whining as he looked around.

"Oh, I see." Emily realized she wasn't the reason for this change, but she was all right with it. "You're not into my stories. You know this route and these streets. You're almost home."

CHAPTER SEVEN

Emily pulled into the driveway of a small home with a tiny patch of yard next to the driveway. There was a bit of fence around the side with a gate, suggesting that at least there was a larger garden in the back for Diesel to run around. The house itself looked like it needed a new coat of paint, and the windows were a bit grubby, but it was nothing that would affect the happiness of the dog.

"You do me a favor, Diesel." Emily unbuckled her seatbelt and turned to her passenger, nose-to-nose with the dog. "You go and have a good life. I know you miss Clark, and I'm so sorry for you for that. But I think you'll still do just fine, and at least you don't have to wonder where you're going to live." She gave him another scratch under the chin before she got out of the car and led him up the walkway to the front door.

Diesel was quickly becoming uncontrollable. He strained at the end of his leash as he hopped up onto his hind legs and slammed his paws into the door. He was ready to get back into his home!

"Hey, buddy! It's all right! Calm down!" The door swung open to reveal a young man who seemed to be of a similar age to Clark. He was tall and athletic in a pair of shorts and a t-shirt, and he immediately bent down to take Diesel into his open arms. "Yeah, I know! What a scare you had, huh? Thought you were going to be in doggie jail forever, didn't you?"

Emily was very sure that Diesel would've knocked Mason straight to the ground if he'd been a weaker man. Still, she was so very glad to know that the dog had a home even though his owner was gone. "Is there anything else you need?" she asked politely. "Ms. Austin told me your car was in the shop, so if you need me to run and get some kibble, I'm happy to do so."

Mason, who seemed to have nearly forgotten she was there in his enthusiasm over the dog, looked up at her in surprise. He got back to his feet and opened the door wider. "I'm so sorry. I completely forgot my manners. Come on in for a minute. I didn't mean to leave you standing out there."

"That's all right. I'm just glad that Diesel is so happy. He didn't like the shelter very much, even though we take excellent care of the animals there. I'm Emily Cherry, by the way." She stepped inside the front room, observing a rather beaten sofa against one wall. Someone was in the habit of holding their drink right on the arm, since several drippy stains ran down the green fabric. The carpet wasn't in much better condition, but there was a massive flatscreen television on another wall. Yes, this was certainly the sort of place being rented by two young men.

"Mason Hailey. I hope Diesel didn't give you too much trouble."

"Not me, anyway," she replied honestly. "I guess he was a bit scared, and they weren't sure if they were going to be able to get him over to you. The two of us got along just fine, though. And I'm so sorry for your loss, by the way. Were you and Clark very close?" She realized her faux pas and hoped that she hadn't embarrassed herself too much. Emily had no way of knowing how long Mason and Clark had been living together, and this whole thing was probably very tragic for him.

Mason's mouth drooped a little as he shrugged, showing that he cared in his own macho way. "Close enough. It's been pretty tough. It's not the kind of thing you ever think about happening."

"I completely understand." Emily hadn't expected her husband's death, nor had she had any reason to. Everything had been fine, until it wasn't. "We have to give ourselves time to process all the feelings that come along with these sorts of events. We can't expect to just cry a little and then be done with it all. I'm sure having Diesel here will help you."

"Yeah, as long as I can stay here anyway," Mason muttered.

"What do you mean?" Emily knew he probably hadn't meant to say that, and she bent down to pet Diesel so she wouldn't have to look Mason straight in the eye.

"Um, nothing. It's just that Clark and I always used to split the rent. I know this house doesn't look like much, but it costs quite a bit just for the two of us to keep it going. I'll have to find a new roommate, but that's not always an easy thing to do. Even Clark wasn't perfect. He was always having money troubles."

"Is that so? That's a shame." Emily's eyes swept through the room. This was where Clark had lived. There very well might be a clue here that could help her figure out what had happened to him. "I only met him briefly, but I always hate to hear when young folks are struggling like that."

"I'm sorry. Please, have a seat." Mason gestured to what she supposed was the prime seat on the sofa, the one with the drippy arm.

Emily obliged, pleased to see that Diesel followed her to her new position and laid his big, blocky head on one of her knees. "I wouldn't think someone who worked at a vet's office would have money issues," she pressed.

Mason parked himself on an armchair a short distance away and braced his elbows on his knees. "He did always manage to come up with his share of the rent, but it was at the eleventh hour every time. He would be sweating bullets, and then he'd make me sweat bullets, too. The landlord doesn't care if I pay my half. He wants the whole thing, and not a pound less."

Her curiosity was piqued, to say the least. She smiled sweetly at Mason. "You kids are so creative these days. I don't know what I'd do if I had to come up with money last minute like that. I guess I'm just not that resourceful." If she were lucky, he'd open up and tell her exactly what it was Clark was up to. She had a sneaking suspicion that blackmail had become a regular hobby of his, but she had no evidence to go on just yet. She wasn't even sure if she'd get it, but she knew she wanted to try.

Diesel had made his way over to Mason now. He'd found a tennis ball under the coffee table and proudly presented it to his new owner. Mason obliged, taking it out of the dog's mouth and throwing it gently down the hall. The big canine went galloping after it.

"Well, you see, Clark was doing fine when the two of us first moved in together. We both had steady jobs, and we worked out exactly how we were going to split the bills. It seemed like a great situation. Then his aunt went into an assisted living home. She couldn't stay on her own anymore, but those places cost a lot of money. The aunt didn't have any children of her own, so Clark felt sort of obligated."

"Oh, that's so sad." Emily pressed her fingers to her jawline, wondering how the cranky clerk Clark could be so sympathetic to the needs of an old woman on her own. It made her wonder if she'd misjudged him in some way.

Mason nodded. "It tore him up, but he sure did everything he could to make sure she could stay where she needed to be. She really liked the home, and it was a good place for her. To get a few quick bucks he'd sell his blood or do some yardwork for a neighbor, but that only lasted so long. The next thing I knew he was diving into one scheme after the next, thinking he could buy a big box of items and sell them wholesale or take a trip to the casino."

Emily shook her head, genuinely confused. "Why not just get a second job, especially if this was an ongoing thing?"

Mason lifted his hands in the air. "That's exactly what I kept asking him. His aunt needed the money every month, and so did he. It would make sense to get something steady, but he just really liked feeling like he got one over on someone else. I never did understand it."

"Who's going to pay for his aunt now?" Emily wondered aloud.

"She passed away about a year ago," Mason explained. Diesel returned with the ball and happily dropped it in his lap. He tossed it down the hall once again.

That was some clarification, but it didn't make the case about Clark any clearer. According to Dr. Cunningham, Clark was blackmailing her just a few months ago. That didn't fit in with the timeline of Clark's aunt needing financial help. "I'm sorry to hear that."

"I thought it would make things a lot easier for him, but he was in too deep by that point. He was just successful enough with all his little ventures that he couldn't seem to get himself back out. He was gambling and getting in trouble with loan sharks. They'd come and knock on the door at all hours of the day and night asking for him. I don't like to admit it, but it was kind of scary." The tennis ball had been returned to him once again, and this time he sent it bouncing off into the kitchen. Diesel scrambled off after it.

"As you should be," Emily replied, feeling rather sorry for Mason. He seemed like a good young man, and she didn't like to think he'd been put into a bad situation. "Do you think these loan sharks had anything to do with his death?"

"I really don't know," Mason admitted. "I'm trying not to think about it too much. I'm just glad that I'm able to take care of Diesel for him. I was freaking out when I heard what happened and nobody knew where Diesel was at first. I can make sure there's one less thing for Clark to worry about." He scrubbed his knuckles over the dog's ears when he came trotting back into the room, proud of himself for having found the ball once again.

"You're a good friend," Emily assured him. "I should get going back to the shelter. There are lots of other cats and dogs who need me, but I'm happy to know there's one less who does. You take care, Diesel, and be a good boy."

He gave her another one of his body wags as Mason let her out the front door.

Emily clucked her tongue as she got back in her car. It was clear that Clark knew how to get himself into trouble, whether it was blackmail, gambling, or loan sharks. It could very well be even more than that. She had to wonder, though, if there was still some other part of his life that she wasn't seeing. Why still go to the trouble of running his little schemes if he was no longer helping his aunt? For that matter, *was* he ever helping a sick aunt? Clark had already tried to extort his former boss, so Emily wouldn't put it past him to lie to his roommate about exactly why he was after more money. She just didn't know if she had any way of finding out for sure.

CHAPTER EIGHT

"I'm so glad you could join me today." Emily gently removed Rosemary's paws from the edge of the table before she set down the tea tray. "I haven't seen you in a while, and I thought it would be nice if the two of us had a little time to chat. Sugar?"

"Yes, please." DC Alyssa Bradley accepted the dainty cup that Emily handed to her. She stirred the hot liquid gently, but her eyes were sharply on Emily. "I was glad to come over. I always enjoy spending time with you, but I have a feeling this isn't a simple friendly visit?"

Emily smiled as she sat down and picked up her own cup. "I'd be lying if I denied what you're saying, and I don't like to consider myself a liar. I have a feeling, however, that it wouldn't go over well with you or anyone else at your office if I flat out told you I wanted to discuss the Clark Gibson case."

"You're right about that," Alyssa agreed. "Chief Inspector Woods has a sharp eye on me. If I so much as forget to cross a t on my reports, he lets me know."

"But that means he's paying attention to what you're doing," Emily pointed out. "He probably wouldn't notice as much if he didn't think you'd amount to something someday." She knew that Alyssa wanted very badly to be Chief Inspector someday, and Emily wanted her to have it. She was a bright young girl, and there was no good reason that she couldn't hold the position once she had a little more experience under her belt.

"I like to think you're right, but only time will really tell. There are any number of other officers who want a chance to move up the ranks, and I'm pretty far down the line at the moment." She took a sip of her tea and frowned into it. She looked like she was about to go on, but then Rosemary jumped up and swiped at her bracelet.

"No, no," Emily chided, scooping up the big fluffy feline and pulling her away before she had a chance to accidentally break the delicate chain. "I don't think Alyssa would want you to do that. You and I can have some time later to work on some crafts. That ought to keep you happy."

"I did see that you've been featuring Rosemary and some other pets on your blog," Alyssa noted with a smile.

"You read it?" Emily felt just as flattered as she did when she'd found out her own children were getting on her website and reading what she wrote. Somehow, that meant so much more than even perfect strangers stumbling across her page and leaving a comment or two.

"Of course, I do!" Alyssa enthused. "I love seeing what you have going on, and of course Rosemary is always the star of the show."

Finding a bit of knotted yarn that was no longer any good for any crochet projects, Emily ran the end of it across the floor for Rosemary to chase. "It was a natural progression, I'd say. She just kept getting into everything while I was crafting, and she's too cute for me to scold her for long. Unfortunately, all this time that I've been spending at the shelter has left her feeling a bit left out." She grinned as Rosemary's pupils widened and she made a wild leap for the yarn, slapping her fluffy paws over it.

"Which brings us right back to Clark Gibson, doesn't it?" Alyssa asked, one eyebrow raised. "You were taking a shelter pet to see Dr. Gallagher when you found Clark deceased."

Emily nodded. "That's right."

"And now I'm guessing you have some other information about the case that you'd like to share with me?" DC Bradley pressed. "We may not be able to say officially what this visit is all about, but my curiosity is really getting the better of me today."

That was something Emily could certainly understand. After all, she wouldn't have asked so many questions of the people she'd seen over the last few days if that wasn't the case for herself as well. "I might. I'm not entirely sure. I keep waiting for something to really fall into place so I can figure out what's happening, but I don't think I have it all yet. Maybe you can start by telling me whether or not I even need to worry. I assume that this case is officially a homicide?"

Alyssa frowned slightly, and Emily knew she was contemplating how much she could say without technically getting herself in trouble. "That's correct."

"All right, then. At least I know I'm not on a wild goose chase." Emily flicked the bit of yarn across the room for Rosemary to play with on her own. "It turns out that Clark Gibson was in trouble with loan sharks."

To her surprise, Alyssa nodded. "We found out about that, actually. It's standard practice for us to look into a person's finances when we have cases like this. Money is often a big motivator in murder, so bank and credit card statements can tell us a lot. There were some odd-looking payments, and we tracked them to a local loan shark."

Rosemary brought the string back, enjoying this impromptu game of fetch. Emily took it from her and tossed it again, realizing she was in the same place as Mason had been when he was playing with Diesel while he talked to her. It was hard to concentrate on just how cute the cat was being when she was so anxious to find out more. "You did? Did you talk to him?"

Alyssa sighed, giving up on whether or not she was supposed to share this information. "We did. I'm happy to say he was pretty cooperative, which isn't what I expected. He explained that Clark would borrow from him regularly, but he never explained what the money was for. The loan shark didn't really care as long as he was making plenty of money in interest. He says most people come to him because they're addicted to gambling, or rather to the idea of winning. Of course, they rarely do."

Emily remembered that Mason had mentioned Clark liked to gamble, but she didn't think that was quite the right track. "I'm assuming this financier, shall we say, had an alibi?"

"A solid one," Alyssa replied with a nod. This time, Rosemary brought the yarn to her. Alyssa obliged, plucking the little bit of yellow string and flicking it over near the window. "He's in the clear, even if he is a little slimy."

Emily tapped her chin. "You said you were looking at his bank statements. Did you happen to see any payments that would correspond with Clark paying for his aunt to stay in an assisted living facility? His former roommate said that's where a lot of his money went. He said this aunt has been deceased for a while, though."

"Ah, that explains that, then." Alyssa picked her cup back up as she saw that Rosemary was now rolling around on the floor underneath the front picture window, tackling the bit of yarn as though it were a giant yellow snake from the Amazon. "We found direct payments to a place called Willowbrook Assisted Living, but not for some time. We weren't sure if they had anything to do with what happened to Clark, but they seemed odd enough that we thought it was worthwhile to investigate. I was going to give them a call today, but you've saved me from having to do that."

"Glad I could help," Emily replied earnestly. She tucked a strand of her brilliant red hair behind her ear. Her eyes rested on Rosemary, but her mind was wandering off in other directions. "I just don't understand. His aunt doesn't need his assistance anymore, but he was continuing to get himself in trouble financially. He had a steady job, and yet it seems that he was probably the one blackmailing Dr. Gallagher." She explained what she'd learned from Dr. Cunningham about her former employee.

Alyssa finished her cup of tea and waved her hand over the rim when Emily asked if she wanted another. "I can't. I have to go in for my shift in a bit. It's interesting, though. Why would he continually put himself in such dire straits? Granted, sometimes folks just get themselves into a rut and don't know how to dig themselves back out again. Or they simply don't want to."

"Dr. Gallagher said he'd stopped paying his blackmailer," Emily mused as she rolled her fingers across the smooth side of her teacup. "Clark needed the money, or at least he felt he did. Could he have been getting less money than he was supposed to from Dr. Gallagher?"

"It's possible. Perhaps Dr. Gallagher knew that Clark didn't have any good references after getting fired from Dr. Cunningham's office. He could get away with paying him less, and that could cause problems for Clark. I do have access to his bank statements, but that's only going to give me a final figure when it comes to his paychecks. I think we need more information than that."

Emily wasn't unhappy to hear this. "I do believe that Millie is due for her next set of shots. I'd be happy to bring you along for my appointment. As long as it won't get you in trouble, of course," she added quickly. "I don't want to do anything that will decrease your chances of getting the promotions you're dreaming of."

"If anything, I think you're helping me far more than you're hindering," Alyssa chuckled. "There are a couple of cases that I'd never have solved without you."

"I think you would have," Emily countered. "You're good at what you do. I'm just a nosy old lady who doesn't know how to mind her own business."

Alyssa laughed again. "Well, it suits you! And you can get away with it. Everyone looks at my uniform and instantly stops talking. They see you and want to catch up like old friends. I'm not complaining, though, not if it all comes down to finding out what really happened and bringing the criminal to justice."

When Alyssa had headed off to work, Emily picked up a small stuffed mouse and dangled it in front of Rosemary's face. "What do you think, sweetheart? Did something bad happen to Clark?"

Rosemary wasn't paying attention to a word she said. She was far more interested in the mouse, and she whacked at it enthusiastically with her paw.

Emily knew that her cat was making some very cute faces that would go beautifully on the blog, but she didn't bother stopping and getting out her camera or even her cell phone. Sweet little Rosemary needed some pure attention all to herself, and she deserved it. Still, Emily's mind simply didn't want to leave Clark Gibson's mysterious death alone. "All I can say is that I hope it doesn't have anything to do with Dr. Gallagher himself. He seems like a sweet old man, and I don't like to think anyone who's that good with animals could be a murderer."

If Rosemary had an opinion on it, she didn't let Emily know. She grabbed the mouse, yanked down hard enough to get it out of Emily's fingers, and sank her teeth into it.

CHAPTER NINE

"We've got an extra stop to make today, Millie. I don't think you'll mind too much once you meet her, though. Alyssa is a very sweet girl. Now, you might not think someone who's tough enough to be a police officer can be sweet, but I promise you that she is. She likes my cat, Rosemary. Of course, who wouldn't?" Emily laughed. She decided she rather liked talking to all the animals she met at Best Friends Furever. It made her feel as though she had a real connection to them while she was caring for them. They deserved that, at the very least.

Millie had gotten a little more used to these car rides after taking several of them with Emily. She sat placidly in her crate with her feet tucked up underneath her chest, looking around curiously.

"Here we are." Emily pulled up in front of the address she'd been given and smiled when Alyssa decided to position Millie's crate on her lap instead of putting her in the back seat. She eyed the short-sleeved blouse and jeans Alyssa wore. "Decided not to go for the uniform today?"

"My badge will be enough," she explained as she buckled in. "I don't want the whole office to be up in arms when they see a police officer come through the door, and it would look a little stranger considering I'm with you. And like I said before, people prefer to talk to me when I'm not in uniform."

"Oh, yes. I do remember you saying that. Personally, I've always found you very pleasant to talk to, no matter how you're dressed." Emily pulled away from the curb and headed for Dr. Gallagher's office.

"That's because you're not being accused of anything," the young officer reminded her.

Emily frowned. "I suppose that's true. You don't think we're actually after Dr. Gallagher today, do you? I mean, he seems like such a nice man. Even if Clark were blackmailing him, it's hard to believe he'd do anything like that." She enjoyed helping Alyssa on her cases when she had a chance. It made her feel important and like she had something to do, but she realized there might be some aspects of it that wouldn't be very pleasant.

Fortunately, Alyssa shook her head of dark hair. "I don't think so. We do need more information, though, and I'm very hopeful that we can get it from him. He was cooperative last time, so that's promising."

Though the place had been closed while the crime scene was being processed, things looked just as they did the first time she'd been to Dr. Gallagher's office, now that it was open again. The little building sat back off the road with a few cars in the lot. There was a woman in the waiting area holding a cat crate protectively on her lap while the gentleman on the other end of the row of chairs was trying hard to keep his dog in control. The big mutt was very curious about what might be inside that carrier, and he was pulling with all his strength against his leash. His dark wet nose kept creeping closer and closer to the carrier door despite his owner's commands to sit. The flash of a claw through the bars finally sent the dog whimpering back to his owner, and several apologies were exchanged.

Emily's stomach was a hard lump when she stepped up to the desk. This was right where she'd seen Clark, both alive and dead. She'd known, of course, that he wouldn't be here, but it was still strange to see Lara sitting in his place.

"Good morning!" she chirped. "How can I help you?"

Well, at least it hadn't affected her work ethic to know that a man had died practically right where she was sitting. "Millie is here for her appointment."

"Great. I'll just get you checked in." Lara's eyes flashed up toward Alyssa out of curiosity but then returned to her computer. "You can have a seat. It'll be just a few moments."

"Thank you." Emily turned to sit, finding that she was stuck putting Millie either very close to a rather curious dog or a rather crabby cat. Neither one sounded like a pleasant experience for the poor shelter cat, who had already gone through enough as far as she was concerned. She'd just resigned herself to standing nearby when a familiar face appeared in the back doorway.

"Millie?" Dr. Gallagher called.

"Here she is," Emily replied with a breath of relief. She and Alyssa followed him down the hallway to the exam room.

The veterinarian flipped through Millie's chart. "Dr. Cunningham's office sent me over the record of what they did while we weren't open, so we're all caught up on that. It'll just be a quick shot and then she'll be on her way. Although this feels like more than a simple visit," he added as he looked openly and curiously at Alyssa.

"I suppose that means you remember me, Dr. Gallagher." Alyssa extended her hand to shake his before she got out her badge. "DC Alyssa Bradley"

Emily felt bad that they'd ambushed the doctor like this. "I'm so sorry that we surprised you this way, Dr. Gallagher. It's just that DC Bradley has a few more questions, and so I let her tag along with me for this appointment. That way you wouldn't have to take any extra time out of your day."

"That's quite all right," he assured her with a thin smile. He occupied his hands by getting Millie out of her crate and then smoothing her dark gray fur back into place. "I told the police before that I'd do everything to help with the investigation, and I meant that."

"We appreciate that. Dr. Gallagher, we've been finding some interesting pieces of information in regard to Clark's finances. Were you aware that he was having financial trouble?"

The vet's eyebrows shot up toward his receding hairline. "This is a small office. When you have only a handful of people working together, you don't have the secretive nature that you do in a big corporate office. We tend to know things about each other, but Clark never shared that with me before."

"You mentioned before that someone was blackmailing you, and that you'd refused to make the most recent payments. How has that been going?"

"Surprisingly well, actually. I was fully expecting some sort of backlash for it, for the blackmailer to finally do what they said they would and release information about my mistake to the public, but—oh." Dr. Gallagher had just opened a drawer to fetch a syringe, but now his hands fell limply on the sides of the drawer instead of reaching inside. His shoulders slumped forward, and he shook his head. "I had no idea," he said quietly. "I suppose that makes sense, though."

Emily felt so sorry for him. He'd only just now realized it was Clark who had been coercing him, and it was hitting him hard. She stroked her fingers around Millie's ears.

"And how is that?" Alyssa pressed. She spoke differently when she was questioning someone, with more authority, and yet she still managed to be gentle. Emily was always impressed by this.

He shook his head once again as he slowly put a syringe together and then opened a cabinet to retrieve a small glass vial. "It would have to be someone who was here, who knew what had happened. I suppose I was really trying to convince myself that it was the patient's owner, because that made the most sense. But Clark was here that day, and so he knew all about it. That's a very frustrating thing, and it's even more difficult for me because I don't like to speak ill of the dead."

"Can you think of any reason that Clark would need to do this? I mean as far as finances? We've been looking into his statements, which gives us some insight, but we'd like to know a little more about how he was getting paid here," Alyssa stated.

Filling the syringe and then making sure that the injection site was clean, Dr. Gallagher nodded. "He earned the same as anyone else here. I admit I don't pay as much as some of the larger office like Dr. Cunningham's, but it's a reasonable rate that we both agreed on when I hired him. I can get you his check stubs if you'd like."

"That would be wonderful. Thank you."

Dr. Gallagher somberly finished with Millie and gave her a scratch on the ears. "I'll be right back."

When he stepped out of the room, Emily turned to Alyssa. "What do you think?"

"I think there's definitely something going on with Clark and his finances that led to his death, but I still can't quite put my finger on it. Rest assured that Dr. Gallagher isn't a prime suspect, if that's what you're concerned about."

"I just feel bad for him," Emily admitted as she put Millie back in the crate. "I feel like we ambushed him, and he was genuinely hurt that Clark had blackmailed him like that." She couldn't even imagine how she would feel if a coworker had done the same to her. In a small place like this, the employees were probably a lot like family.

"It would've been a surprise for me to talk to him either now or at another time. Nobody likes having to talk to the police, whether they know it's coming or not. And honestly, it's usually better if they don't. Even the innocent ones tend to get in their own heads and think too much about what they're going to say if they're given enough time."

"I suppose that's true."

"Here you are." Dr. Gallagher returned and handed a manilla envelope to DC Bradley, still looking grim. "Please let me know if you need anything else. Oh, and Millie should be all good to go now. I hope she finds a new home soon."

"Thank you."

They headed out into the front lobby, and Emily stopped at the desk. "I'm sorry to bother you, but Ms. Austin was needing to get a balance on the charge account for Best Friends Furever, please."

Lara beamed. "Not a problem at all. I can look that right up for you."

"Excuse me, miss?" A young man stepped up to the counter. He had a fat little puppy with a curly tail on a leash. "I'm so sorry to say this, but my dog made a mess on the floor. Do you have some paper towels so I can clean it up?"

"It's all right! It happens all the time!" Lara said with a laugh and a brilliant smile. She turned back to Emily. "Give me just one second, please."

"Sure." Emily waited patiently while Lara stepped away from the desk to get some cleaning supplies. Her eyes wandered around, wondering how many things had changed now that Clark wasn't' here. Had he made much of an impact on the office? Would they really miss him? Dr. Gallagher likely didn't, considering what Clark had done to him. It was such a shame to be so young and have your whole life ahead of you, only to leave behind a legacy of blackmail and greed.

Her gaze drifted down to the countertop in front of her, where a large desk calendar rested just in front of the computer monitor. Client appointments were probably kept in the system, since this calendar wasn't the right kind for that, but holidays and doodles had been marked on it. Emily spotted the day that she'd come in and found Clark dead. It said, 'Howard Family Reunion.' She remembered that Dr. Gallagher had told Chief Inspector Woods that he was at a family reunion. It was too bad that had gotten ruined for him.

CHAPTER TEN

Emily hurriedly trotted over to the front door as soon as she heard a car pull into the driveway. Sensing that something exciting was happening, Rosemary scampered along at her heels. Emily peeked through the curtains, seeing exactly what she thought she would. "You're going to have so much fun, Rosemary! Or at least, I hope you will!" She opened the door a moment later to let Mavis in.

"How is he?" Emily asked excitedly, catching a glimpse of white fur through the mesh in the soft-sided carrier her daughter had in her hands. "Has he been adjusting well?"

Mavis laughed. "Mom, I think you've asked me that every day since I adopted him! But yes, he's doing just fine. I hope he'll get along well with Rosemary."

"There's only one way to find out." Emily clasped her hands in front of her as she waited for Mavis to set the carrier down and unzip it. Mavis had adopted Gus after she'd met him at the Best Friends Furever booth that'd been set up at a craft fair. She had been the last person Emily would've expected to want a cat, but it sounded as though things were going well.

As soon as a hole big enough opened up, Gus popped his head out. His fur was snowy white save for the pale orange splotches on his face, tail, and feet. His bright blue eyes scanned the room and quickly landed on Rosemary. His ears twitched, and then he wiggled his way out of the carrier and came straight across to rug to the other cat.

Rosemary looked alarmed for a moment, taking a few steps backward and twitching her tail awkwardly. Gus was far less concerned. He marched straight forward and began sniffing her.

"Here, kitties." Emily picked up a box of cat toys that she'd put in the living room for just this purpose, figuring that if they had something to do, they would have a better chance of getting along. Cat playdates might make Mavis come over more often, and Emily always loved having her children around. She rolled a couple of small plastic balls with jingle bells inside towards the cats, pleased to see that they immediately began batting them around.

"I think you've got them all figured out," Mavis stated as she sat down on the sofa. "I worry that Gus gets too lonely while I'm at work."

Emily sat down next to her, laughing a little as Gus lost his ball under the wingback chair and pressed his face underneath it to find it again. "He might, but I think cats are pretty resilient. Rosemary has been a little miffed at me for suddenly spending time at the shelter, but that's because she's used to me being at home. You've been working the whole time you've had Gus."

"That's true. Speaking of the shelter, it seems like you must be getting on quite well there. I've seen all the pet photos you've been posting. I'm glad I already have Gus, or else you'd make me run right over to Best Friends Furever and get another pet with those sweet stories!"

"That's very kind of you." Emily felt her cheeks warm. She appreciated the praise, of course, but it was really more about the connection to her daughter. "It's been rewarding work, both what I do at the shelter and what I do about the blog."

"And your little trip to the vet's office?" Mavis asked, raising one eyebrow. "I haven't called to pester you about it, because I know you don't want any of us fussing over you, but that can't have been easy."

"No," Emily admitted. "It wasn't, because it wouldn't be for anyone. I'm doing fine, though, if that's what you're worried about."

"Are you sure?" her daughter asked as Gus went racing by, chasing the ball he'd recovered from under the chair. "You look like you've got something on your mind."

Emily pressed her lips together. She had been trying to find out everything she could about Clark's death. She knew that Mavis wouldn't be happy about that, and the last thing she needed was her daughter to chide her over what sort of behavior was all right for an older woman. Emily wasn't sure, though, that she wanted to hold anything back. It was her life, after all, and her kids didn't have to like it. "I do. You see, this young man, Clark Gibson, was in some serious financial trouble. I'm quite sure that has something to do with his death, but I haven't been able to figure out how. It seemed that he was threatening others. He'd even blackmailed his own boss!"

"That doesn't sound like a good long-term plan," Mavis noted.

Rosemary abandoned the ball she was chasing and went after Gus instead, making a cute little trill in her throat as she captured the tip of his tail between her paws. She hadn't used her claws at least, considering that Gus sprang away from her, only to turn around and pounce right back. The two of them were definitely having fun.

"I completely agree, and I just don't understand." Emily balled her hand into a fist and tapped it on her knee. "Dr. Gallagher had hired him despite the fact that he'd been fired from another veterinary office. He gave him a chance, and I doubt there would be many people who would. They were a small office, just three of them as far as I could tell, and they had to be like family." She paused, just about to pound her fist against her leg again.

"What is it?" Mavis asked, ignoring Gus as he crashed into the door of the coat closet. The cat was fine, considering the way he and Rosemary turned right around and began hunting the same catnip mouse. "Are you okay?"

"Yes. It's just that I've thought about something." It couldn't really be all that significant, she was sure. After all, it was just a few words scribbled on a piece of paper. If it did mean anything, then why would it have been left out for all the world to see? "The day that I took Millie in for her shots, Dr. Gallagher wasn't there. He was at a family reunion."

"All right," Mavis said patiently, waiting for the other shoe to drop.

"It was marked on the office calendar as 'Howard Family Reunion.'"

"Must've been on his mother's side of the family."

"Yes," Emily nodded, "but why mark that on the calendar that's for the whole office, even if there were only three people who worked there? Why not put that Dr. Gallagher is off work? Wouldn't that make more sense?"

Mavis frowned. "I suppose it would. You did say it was a small office, though, and they were like family. Before I worked at my current firm, I was at that much smaller place on the other side of town. We usually knew exactly what our coworkers were taking off for, whether they had a doctor's appointment, or their kid had an event."

"Yes, but two of them were out of the office that day." Emily wondered how she hadn't thought about it before. If Dr. Gallagher was at a family reunion, then where was the other vet tech, Lara? Why was Clark left there all by himself? Could Lara and the doctor be related?"

Mavis leaned forward. She braced her elbow on her knees and tapped her fingers against her chin as she watched the cats roll and tumble across the rug. "We need to call Genevieve."

"What?" Emily's fingers nearly slipped and made her drop her teacup. It was just such an unexpected idea. "What does she have to do with any of this?"

"Nothing yet, but the best place I can think of to figure out what the connection between the two of them may be is social media. I could go down to my office and probably find a way to hack into all sorts of records—"

"Mavis…" Emily scolded.

"—but I know I could get in trouble for things like that, and so I'm not going to. Genevieve, however, has her finger on the very pulse of social media itself." Mavis was already dialing. "If anyone can find out, it's her."

It didn't take long to get Genevieve on the phone, and Mavis put her on speaker so they could both talk to her as she quickly explained the situation. "It may not be significant to the case at all, but if we could figure out whether or not the two of them are related, it would at least be some more information."

"Ooo, I get to help solve a murder? I'm all in on that!" Genevieve practically squealed. "Give me a second here. The veterinary office has their own page, so that's a good start. Aha, yes, and here's the good doctor himself. Doesn't look like he posts very much, and someone really needs to teach him how to take better photos."

"Not really the point, Genny," Mavis reminded her.

"Right, right. Okay, you said Lara is the person we're looking for? Does she have a last name?"

Mavis looked to Emily, but she shook her head. "I don't know what it is."

"That's all right. I'm sure I can find her anyway. People always link themselves to their family and other things they're interested in, so it won't be hard. I have a Lara Barnett who lists her place of work as Gallagher Veterinary Medicine."

"That must be her!" Mavis enthused.

"That doesn't prove they're related, though," Emily interjected, already starting to wonder if anything like this could possibly work, "only that they work in the same place, which I know."

"But that's where you have to start," Genevieve explained. "You find the connection that's already in place, and then you can expand out from there. It's exactly how I find people in the fashion industry. If I already know a designer, then I can reach out to other people who know her. And look here, I have a public post from Lara to Dr. Gallagher that says, 'Happy Birthday, Uncle Melvin!' That's it! They're definitely related! Anything else I can dig up for you ladies?"

"You did it, Genny! You're awesome! What do you think, Mum? Anything else?"

Emily knew she should be rejoicing in the simple fact that they'd discovered another piece of information, but it wasn't quite sitting right with her. She shook her head so that Mavis could get off the phone with Genevieve.

"What's wrong?" Mavis asked when she'd hung up.

"Simply knowing they're related doesn't necessarily tell me anything, and I know there's got to be something I'm missing. I'll call Alyssa later and let her know. She's the detective, after all. I'm sure she'll figure out if this is important or not." Emily absently watched as the cats ran into the kitchen and then right back out again.

"Call her right now." Mavis picked up Emily's cell phone and handed it to her. "I won't mind."

Emily reluctantly took the phone, realizing she'd been worried about making her own daughter jealous of the time she was spending with Alyssa. "Are you sure?"

"Mom, it's important to you. That's the only thing that matters to me. Call her up and tell her what we found out.

You'll never know until you do."

She was right, and Emily definitely wanted to know. As she listened to the ringing on the other end of the line, she hoped this was something more significant than it felt. Otherwise, she'd just be wasting Alyssa's time.

CHAPTER ELEVEN

Jefferson jumped and barked at the end of his leash as Emily got him out of his kennel and marched him up the long hallway toward the door. The other dogs along the way with whom he'd made friends during his stay here, shouted their congratulations and their jealousy from their own pens. It was both sad and wonderful, but Emily chose to concentrate on the happy part.

"Are you ready?" she asked the little terrier mix as she brought him out of the noisy kennel and they moved down the next hallway toward the lobby. "Things are going to be very different for you from now on. It's going to take a little bit of adjusting, but I know you can do it. Just hang in there and remember how much your new family loves you." Tears welled up in her eyes just thinking about how he was about to go home to a new place.

When she opened the final door into the lobby, noise exploded all over again. Two children jumped up out of their chairs, quickly abandoning the cell phones and tablets they'd brought along for entertainment while their parents filled out all the boring paperwork. They were down on their knees on the hard floor, each vying for as much attention from Jefferson as possible. The little dog barked happily as he trotted back and forth between the two of them, absorbing all the pets he could get.

"There's our boy!" Mr. Brown whooped, just as excited as his kids were. "Did I tell you that he looks just like the dog I had as a kid?"

Lily Austin smiled warmly at him. "You did, and I think he'll be a wonderful choice for your family. I think you've got everything you need in this envelope, including a copy of his vet records and information about the vet that we use, if you'd like to go to the same one. Please do keep in mind that if he doesn't work out for your family for any reason, you can bring him back."

"I don't think that'll be a problem," Mrs. Brown said as she took the envelope. "We've all been so enchanted by Jefferson. The kids fell in love with how cute and playful he is, and of course my husband loves the memory he brings back. For me, I just couldn't resist it once I'd read his story online. Whoever you have doing your blog is fantastic."

"Actually, we don't have a blog ourselves," Lily explained. "Our volunteer Emily, however, has been putting the animal's stories out there on her blog. Perhaps that's where you read it."

"Oh, it must be! A friend had forwarded me the link, and I didn't even pay attention. How nice to meet you!" Mrs. Brown shook Emily's hand. "I sat at my desk and cried my eyes out after reading about how Jefferson had been abandoned in an old apartment building. I just couldn't stand it, and now here we are!"

"Thank you so much for reading it," Emily replied, thinking she just might get a little choked up herself. "I believe their stories help make people understand that they're more than just property."

"You're absolutely right," Mrs. Brown agreed. "Will you be posting more stories like that? I'll be sure to share them if you do."

Emily knew that the focus of her blog had already shifted a few times, and lately she'd even abandoned crafting in order to write about Rosemary and the pets at the shelter. It was a worthwhile cause, though, and one she wasn't going to give up. Right then and there, she decided that she could fit pet posts in no matter what the subject matter was supposed to be. "I definitely will."

The Browns headed off with Jefferson happily in tow, and her heart was fluttering just as quickly as his little tail.

"That's what I live for," Lily said with a contented sigh. She looked dreamy and relaxed as she looked out the front doors, but then she quickly straightened up. "But not this. I guess Animal Control must have picked up another one for us."

Emily looked over her shoulder to see a uniformed officer coming in, but she smiled. "Hi, Alyssa. Lily, this is DC Alyssa Bradley. Alyssa, this is Lily Austin, the director here."

Alyssa extended her hand. "It's very nice to meet you. Ms. Cherry, could I speak to you for a moment in private?"

"Of course. You don't mind if the dogs listen in, do you? I've got an empty cage that needs to be cleaned out in preparation for its next tenant."

"Lead the way."

They headed back into the kennels. It was loud at first while the dogs took a moment to adjust to Alyssa's presence, but Emily had gotten used to that being the way of things around here. "Sorry for the noise. They'll calm down in a minute."

"That's all right." As Emily stopped at the cage that'd formerly held Jefferson, Alyssa bent down in front of the one next door. She poked her fingers through the wires at the brown dog in the back corner, but he didn't come up to greet her. He lay with his chin on the floor, staring up at her sadly. "Who's this?"

"That's Walter," Emily explained. She knew all the animals by heart at this point, and she was proud of it even if their stories were sad. "He's a bit of an older fellow, probably about ten or so. His family decided they were going to move, and they said they didn't have any room for him."

"So, they just gave him up?" Alyssa's mouth flew open.

Emily nodded sadly as she got a broom and swept up the last bits of Jefferson's fur. "They did. He's been moping ever since. You're welcome to open the door and talk to him, but he hasn't' responded to anyone yet."

Alyssa lifted the latch and swung open the door. The dog still didn't move, but she waited patiently. "I thought I should come by and tell you just how big of a hint you managed to throw my way in finding out that Lara Barnett and Dr. Gallagher were related."

"Oh?" Emily glanced at her through the chain link that separated the two cages, still hoping that the vet wasn't the one in trouble. "What happened?"

"Well, I wasn't sure at first if it would mean much, but I started to look at the evidence we'd gathered, given that context. I also decided to bring Lara in for questioning. She's the only one we hadn't really talked to because she wasn't at the office that day." Alyssa began inching her way across the floor of Walter's cage.

"Because she was at a family reunion?" Emily asked. She moved the food and water dishes out of the cage and set

86

them in a nearby utility sink, where they would be sanitized before the next dog used them.

"Exactly. Of course, it's not a crime to go to her family function. She started to crack when I began asking her about Clark blackmailing her uncle. She just sort of froze over. It's a reaction I've seen people get when they realize they've been caught. They go numb sometimes because they know there's nothing they can do to make it better."

"So, she knew it was Clark?" Emily wished the girl would've just said something about it in the first place. It would've saved them all a lot of headaches.

Alyssa nodded as she held out the back of her hand for Walter to sniff. The gray fur around his nose twitched as he obliged. "She did. Dr. Gallagher was incredibly distressed at the idea of his practice being slandered. The anxiety over it was even causing him some health problems. Lara was livid, and she told Clark he had to stop. He laughed her off, telling her there was no way he was going to give up free money."

Emily clicked her tongue as she filled a mop bucket. "I guess it's not much different than gambling. He was addicted to the thrill of getting money out of people without having to work for it."

"That's the conclusion that I've come to as well, even though we can't ask him if there was any other reason." Alyssa was now brushing her fingers gently over Walter's head, and he thumped his tail placidly against the concrete floor.

Leaving the mop rather wet so it would do a good job of washing the floor, Emily began pushing it around Jefferson's cage. "Am I correct, then, in assuming Lara was the one who poisoned Clark?"

"She put it in his coffee," the young investigator explained. "He was the only one who drank it, so there was no danger of either herself or Dr. Gallagher getting poisoned if she put it in the can of fresh grounds. She didn't even have to put it directly in his cup, which made that easier for her. She's admitted to all of it, and we have her in custody."

Relief washed down over Emily's shoulders. "It's a sad situation, but I'm glad that it at least has come to a conclusion. Now everyone can sleep peacefully at night."

"I'm not sure that I will."

Emily looked up from her mopping to see that Alyssa was on the floor of Walter's cage. He had his head in her lap, and his eyes were closed as she stroked his head. The big old dog looked like he was in heaven. "Oh, my. Someone likes you."

"I think I like him, too. I know he's well taken care of here, but I don't think I can leave him." Alyssa looked up with tears in her eyes. "Would you mind bringing me the paperwork? I don't even want to leave him long enough to go to the front."

Emily leaned her broom against the wall and stepped out. "It would be my pleasure."

THANK YOU FOR CHOOSING A PUREREAD BOOK!

We hope you enjoyed the story, and as a way to thank you for choosing PureRead we'd like to send you this free Special Edition Cozy, and other fun reader rewards...

Click Here to download your free Cozy Mystery
PureRead.com/cozy

Thanks again for reading.
See you soon!

OTHER BOOKS IN THIS SERIES

If you loved this story and want to follow Emily's antics in other fun easy read mysteries continue **dive straight into other books in this series...**

Read them all...

A Troubling Case Of Murder On The Menu

A Crafty Case Of Murder At The Fair

OUR GIFT TO YOU

AS A WAY TO SAY THANK YOU WE WOULD LOVE TO SEND YOU THIS SPECIAL EDITION COZY MYSTERY FREE OF CHARGE.

Our Reader List is 100% FREE

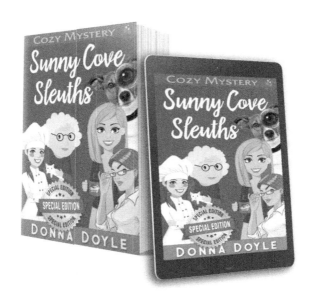

Click Here to download your free Cozy Mystery
PureRead.com/cozy

At PureRead we publish books you can trust. Great tales without smut or swearing, but with all of the mystery and romance you expect from a great story.

Be the first to know when we release new books, take part in our fun competitions, and get surprise free books in your inbox by signing up to our Reader list.

As a thank you you'll receive this exclusive Special Edition Cozy available only to our subscribers...

Click Here to download your free Cozy Mystery
PureRead.com/cozy

Thanks again for reading.
See you soon!

Made in the USA
Coppell, TX
29 October 2023

23577796R00059